ONE OF TH

WESLEY'S ESSEX COLLECTION

HAUNTED CLACTON

A COLLECTION OF GHOSTLY STORIES AND MYSTERIES

WESLEY H. DOWNES

£3.95

Copyright © W. H. Downes. 1992.

ISBN: 0 9519289 0 2.

All Rights Reserved
No part of this publication may be reproduced, stored in a retrieval system, or transmitted in any form without prior written permission from the publisher.

Published by Wesley's Publications, 61 Lymington Avenue, Clacton-on-Sea, Essex CO15 4QE.

First Published 1992.

Printed by Guild Press (Clacton), Clacton-on-Sea, Essex.
Typesetting: Essex Phototypesetting, Clacton-on-Sea, Essex.
Front cover design by Rose Bishop.

AUTHOR'S ACKNOWLEDGEMENTS

I am greatly indebted to all who have contributed stories and information so freely to me, and duly acknowledge the authors of previously published works.
I also wish to thank those who have assisted generally in reading and correcting the manuscript.
Special thanks to Malcolm Batty for his drawings.

INTRODUCTION

Generally, the Clacton area is not credited with being a haunt for Ghosts, (pardon the pun). But, when one spends a little time looking around and asking a few oblique questions, it is surprising what information can be gathered on the subject.

Nowadays the subject of Ghosts and Hauntings is quite acceptable, but this has not always been so — only during this last twenty years has it been possible to discuss the subject openly; prior to this, in lots of households the matter was strictly taboo. This attitude led to either a complete block on information regarding actual 'happenings', or greatly exaggerated stories, usually designed to scare — such as clanking chains, ear-piercing screams or ghosts that injure or even kill anyone who sets eyes on them.

On the latter point, in over forty years of research on the subject, I have never yet found any evidence of anybody actually hearing rattling chains, screams or even being hurt by a ghost — scared yes, but never hurt. Even where there is Poltergeist activity — things get moved, sometimes thrown through the air with some force and there have been many near misses but, so far, no substantiated reports of injury.

But this book is not intended to even scare the reader, just to enlighten them on often unexplained happenings that have occurred in and around Clacton over the years.

I hope that you will enjoy reading this book.

Sleep Well.

W.H.D.

CONTENTS

CLACTON

The Ghosts of Wilson House	Page 6
Haunted Old Carr's Farm House	8
The St. Osyth Road Haunting	10
A Strange Story from a House in Ellis Road	12
The Tragic Story of June ————	15
The Haunted Sweet Shop	20

GT. CLACTON

Unexplained Forces	22
The Haunted Cottages	23
The Room with a View	24
The Ship Inn	25
Treasure Holt	26
The Ghostly Monk	29
The Haunted Restaurant	31
The Apparitions in the Flat	33
The Phantom Horse	34
The Plough Inn Mysteries	35
The Surprise in the Garden	36
The Swinging Highwayman	37

LT. CLACTON

The Haunted Churchyard	38
The Holland Road Figures	39
The Laughing Policeman	40

ST. OSYTH

The Legend of St. Osyth	41
More St. Osyth Hauntings	42

THORPE-LE-SOKEN

The Haunted Bell Inn	43
The Haunted Police Station	45
The Chained Man	47
The Mysterious 'Thing'	47

WEELEY

The Haunted Manor House	48

HOLLAND-ON-SEA

The Randy Ghost	49
The Phantoms of Holland Haven	49
The Mystery and Ghost of Pork Lane	50

WALTON-ON-THE-NAZE

The Sea Captain	52
Other Walton Hauntings	53

KIRBY-LE-SOKEN

Tales of The Red Lion	55

GREAT BENTLEY

The Ghostly Outrider	57

BRADFIELD

The Sandeman Port Ghost	58

Future Reading	60

THE GHOSTS OF WILSON HOUSE

Until a few years ago there was a girls private day and boarding school in Leas Road, Clacton, known as St. Monica's School.

As the number of boarding pupils increased it became necessary to obtain extra accommodation, so the nearby ancient farmhouse known as Alton Park was purchased and renamed Wilson House.

Wilson House may not mean very much to the ordinary reader, but had you been a schoolgirl or a teacher at St. Monica's School, there is little doubt that it would mean a lot, in more ways than one. To some it would bring back pleasant memories of a part of their school life, but to others a cold shiver would run up and down their spines.

Dating back even before 1086, Alton Park was recorded in Domesday Book and over the years has played its part in local history and continued to do so until 1953. When, as stated above, the property was sold to St. Monica's School and was renamed Wilson House after Bishop Henry Wilson, a founder of the School and chairman of the Board of Governors, the house was mainly used as a dormitory for the young ladies who were boarders at the school.

It was at this period of time that various stories of hauntings started to circulate. It is a well known fact that when children reach the age of puberty, especially females, they seem to attract all types of psychic phenomena. It is widely believed that some psychic force is either given off or taken from them at this age, so it is not really surprising that there should be some manifestations occurring when there are several girls of this age together in an old building which had already seen its share of troubles over the years.

To mention all the alleged 'goings on' here would no doubt fill a book of its own, but to get some idea of what the girls saw and heard is very nicely summed up in the following poem composed with the help of some of the past residents of Wilson House.

THE GHOSTS OF WILSON HOUSE

So many nights we've lain awake,
And heard the beams and floorboards shake,
And listened to the moans and groans,
Of ghosts, and grinding bones.

There is no peace in West 8 dorm,
Especially when the night is warm,
For through the window in the night,
Appears a lady dressed in white;
And Hobnail Boots above is heard,
When all the rats and bats are stirred;
Or if in North you've ever slept,
And from your bed you've softly crept
to see beyond the open door —
William — pace the corridor.

On Halloween, when night is young,
On the large meat hook the Butler's hung,
And you'll hear his cries borne through the air —
Its enough to raise a prefects hair!

Once William killed his master's wife
With sharp and cruel and bloody knife;
He killed the lady dressed in white,
At Halloween about midnight.

When Hobnail Boots his neck had wrung,
Across the hook his body slung —
In anger at his cruel deed;
Yet from his sin he's ne'er been freed.

But — "Oh to be in Wilson",
So many girls have cried
Yet maybe they would change their minds
If ever they had tried;
With clanking chains and grinding bones,
And footsteps in the night,
And moans and groans, and wailings,
When you've turned out the lights.

The above poem is dedicated to the girls of St. Monica's Boarding School, Clacton-on-Sea, who tried to sleep in Wilson House.

Wilson House (Alton Park) was demolished in the 1970's and a new house erected on the site.

THE HAUNTED OLD CARR'S FARMHOUSE

The old Carr's Farm House in Coppins Road is over 250 years old and still going strong, in fact when it was put up for sale in the 1970's it was advertised as being complete with resident ghost. Perhaps it should have more correctly read 'its ghosts'.

One evening, the then owner's wife returned home to find their 15 year old daughter sitting terrified in the kitchen, their cat standing beside her with its back arched, fur bristling, its reddish yellow eyes blazing. They had heard footsteps walking across the floor of the bedroom over the kitchen. Knowing that the rest of the family were out, the poor girl just sat tight and waited for someone to return home, in fact, she was far too frightened to move.

Since that evening these footsteps have been heard several times, they always seem to move slowly and softly with no regular timing.

Sometime later, some friends stayed overnight and a temporary bed was put up in the kitchen for them, they were not told of any unusual happenings in the house, but the next morning when asked how they had slept, they replied that they had slept well, but kept being woken up by footsteps above. Thinking that the owner or his wife slept in that room themselves and were possibly having a bad night they made a joke of it, but they were assured that neither of them had got out of bed all night. They were then told of the phantom footsteps that were frequently heard in the kitchen but strangely enough never heard in the actual bedroom.

There is a story that a young servant girl who worked at the old farmhouse was found drowned in the well close to the back door under mysterious circumstances. Could there be any connection between the drowning and the haunting ? Was the girl attacked in that bedroom and then drowned in the well to keep her quiet ?? The secret may never be revealed.

The present owners have also heard startled cries from the area around the top of the stairs, these have been the stifled cries of a young woman and are usually followed by the sounds of a struggle. Could it possibly be a re-enactment of the last moments of the poor young maids life??

At other times, voices of young children have been heard coming from two of the bedrooms, but as soon as anyone approaches these rooms the sounds stop.

One day in 1990, the writer interviewed a young lady who used to live in the old farmhouse and she related some of her personal experiences.

She lived in Carr's Farmhouse with her parents and sister from the age of eight until she was about nineteen. During that time she experienced numerous sightings, and many times heard children talking and laughing in one of the bedrooms, and on a few occasions she also heard the screams of an older girl coming from the top of the stairs, these screams sounded like a girl in pain.

At various times from her bedroom at the rear of the building, she was able to see through to one of the front bedrooms and see a girl of about fourteen years of age, other times there was a younger girl about nine years old, who had long brown hair, sometimes she could clearly hear children talking and playing, also children's footsteps running about.

Sometimes she heard music and singing, yet there was no radio switched on or anything to account for it.

Another time, from her bedroom she clearly heard voices coming from outside her window, these were voices of two men talking in an old style of English, they would have been standing in an area near to an old well.

It was near to this well, that her dog absolutely refused to go near when it was on a lead, it pulled away violently, as if there was something there that it could either see or feel, but whatever it was, it certainly put fear into the dog.

Inside the lounge of the house, there is an old inglenook fireplace with a cupboard on either side. From one of these cupboards she saw two men in red uniforms removing a man who had been hiding in there and it would appear that this man was the local highwayman whose name was Bocking. It is said that he was later hanged from an old elm tree at the junction of the main road from Clacton to St.Osyth and Little Clacton, this area is now known as Bockings Elm. Legend has it, that Bocking was buried beneath the spread of this tree.

There was an occasion when she clearly heard every one of the doors of the kitchen units, which were all fitted with magnetic catches, being opened and shut, yet when she looked in the kitchen there was nothing to be seen.

THE ST OSYTH ROAD HAUNTING

In 1975 there was a house in St. Osyth Road, Clacton, that suddenly became haunted. It had been just an ordinary semi-detached house, occupied by just ordinary people, until one day suddenly without any apparent reason, it all started to happen.

The young couple together with their four year old son had lived there for some six months with no inkling as to what would happen over the next two years.

It all began when the young boy started talking to what they thought was an imaginary girl friend when he was alone in his bedroom. After some time, his mother decided to listen outside his door and she was amazed to hear not only her son's voice, but also the voice of a young girl. When the mother asked about his little friend, the boy said that her name was Georgina.

Another time when his mother was having a bath, she heard the sound of a young girl singing. It was, she said, the most beautiful voice that she had ever heard. But as soon as she moved towards the bathroom door, the singing stopped.

Other phenomenon also happened in the house — household articles would disappear only to re-appear later in their normal places. Once, the mother clearly heard her name being called, but when she turned round to where she thought the voice came from there was nobody there.

Most of these strange happenings occurred whilst her husband was working on night shift at a local factory, but there was one occasion when her husband was there, it was Christmas Day. A black cat mysteriously appeared in their living room, it roamed about for over an hour, then just as mysteriously disappeared, where it came from and where it went they just did not know, all the doors and windows were shut!!!

One night when the husband was asleep in bed, he was suddenly woken up by what appeared to be 'a clammy grip tightening on his shoulder', it was all very frightening, he said.

Two baby-sitters were terrified one night by footsteps moving about the house, and they both felt that there was somebody else in the house.

Other things that occurred at odd times — a musical box suddenly started to play with nobody in the room, banging noises as if someone was hitting the wall, thumping noises occurred both up and down stairs but, the final straw was in January 1978, when at 3 a.m. their bed began to bounce up and down, and a loud banging began on the ceiling and walls, plaster fell from the ceiling. All this went on for some 45 minutes, then just as all seemed to quieten down, heavy footsteps were heard walking about the upstairs rooms.

All this was too much for the family, they decided that the next day they would get in touch with the Bishop of Colchester and ask for his advice.

Eventually a service to exorcise the house was held, which apparently proved to be successful as no further haunting activity has been reported since.

The house was built during the 1890's and as far as can be ascertained nothing untoward has ever happened before, so why it should all have happened during the 3 year period remains an unsolved mystery.

****

ANCIENT BELIEFS

The Romans used to bury food with their dead, — eggs, meat, and oysters to help them on their way — their ghosts come out to see who nicked the wine!!

The ancient Egyptians also buried food, wine, and other personal items with their dead and in some cases even their personal slaves were sealed up alive in the tombs so that they could still serve their masters in the hereafter. It was their belief that the food and drink provided were not so much for their spiritual journey, as for when they eventually returned!

A STRANGE STORY FROM A HOUSE IN ELLIS ROAD

In October 1970, a letter was received from a lady in Ellis Road, Clacton-on-Sea, relating to a series of strange personal experiences; extracts from her letter follow :-

When I was small my family used to call me Gypsy. I used to be able to tell them when anything bad was going to happen. I was born in May ————.

A few years ago I had Duodenal Ulcers and a Doctor tried to get me to go into hospital. I was so scared, I had a feeling I'd die. One night I was very bad and when the Doctor came he warned me if I had another attack, it would be too late, as we lived a long way from Epping Hospital. I had a small son and I didn't want to leave him. This night as I was very bad, I went to bed. It must have been 2 o'clock in the morning when I woke up with a start. I heard someone calling my name. I sat up in bed and although it was summer, the room was icy cold and there was a queer smell like a damp murky tunnel with a faint smell of mushrooms.

I was in a cold sweat, I opened my eyes — there beside the bed I saw my father — I couldn't tell you what his body looked like, but his face was very plain. Although he had been dead for seven years having died in Australia, he looked the same as I saw him last. He said to me "Don't worry Gyp. you'll be alright". He hadn't called me that since I was a kid and I hadn't talked to him for years as we didn't get on.

I grabbed my husband by his hair, he woke up swearing. I was scared as I did it. I saw a grey shadow go towards the window. Then my husband sat up and I turned on the light, he said "My God. What a smell in here — like someone dead.."

I told him what had happened. He laughed and said that I was dreaming. He said that I was as grey as a ghost. The next day he said that the room must be damp, we pulled out the wardrobe, the smell was still there, he said that he'd pull up the floor — which he did, but there was no sign of damp anywhere.

In three days I went into hospital — funny, I wasn't scared any more. The smell went in a week — he couldn't make it out. He told people, but they laughed.

I got over the operation and for a few years, things went well. One night I saw my brother who had been killed in an accident, another time I dreamed my niece had lost her baby, I didn't even know she was having one. Then I had a letter from my sister telling me her daughter had lost her baby.

Two years ago (1968), my son had been in a lot of trouble with the Police, everything now seemed to have gone quiet and he was getting a £50 suit made. My son had made his first date to take a girl out to a dance at the Westcliff Hotel. The tailor had promised to have the suit made for weeks, but kept putting him off. On the Monday before that I went to bed early, my son had the front room, I had the next one, it had glass doors leading to the yard.

Although it was pretty late, I felt restless and it was some time before I eventually fell asleep. Then I woke with a start, I was shaking like a leaf, it was neither dark nor light, I was afraid to open my eyes, I felt as if I was in a cold draught. I opened my eyes and looked to the doors — they were open, then I can't really describe what I saw — I tremble when I think of it — it was like someone with a black cape on, with arms and shoulders, with a head and no face. It seemed to rise up about six feet, it came towards me, bending towards me. I crouched up in the corner, the bed was near the wall, I screamed, it disappeared. My son rushed in with the dog, Sheba jumped on the bed, her hair was all bristled up. I told him what happened — he laughed at me and said it was a dream.

The next night I took a sleeping tablet. For the rest of the week I knew that something was going to happen. On the Saturday night I had to work, I pleaded with my son to be careful, he said if his suit wasn't ready, he'd get drunk. All night while I was working I knew something was going to happen.

I'll make this short, his suit wasn't ready — he got that drunk, the police picked him up. I bailed him out, it was 3 a.m. when we went home, I went to bed. He always got himself something to eat when he came home, he didn't smoke. I always left my matches out for him, this night I didn't. He turned on the oven and grill, he was that drunk, he collapsed. The dog woke me up. I don't know whether I turned off the gas or he came to and turned them on again, anyway the Police came. He was nearly dead. The Police were wonderful, they fought for half an hour and brought him back to life.

Since then I sent him back to Australia where he is doing well, but I always knew when he was in trouble.

P.S. I am reluctant to go in to that room, if I do, I get a terrible feeling, I feel as if I am being watched. I keep the door shut, now I am on my own with just my dog, it is terrible, there is something about the room. I don't know, I haven't seen or heard anything since. I often lay awake to see if I can see my Dad again, but never do. I know I will if anything happens to my son.

ODD HAUNTINGS

There is said to be a ghost who appears on the site of the old Butlins Holiday Camp near the Martello Tower. It is thought to be that of a soldier killed in a fight in the ballroom when it was a Holiday Camp.

****

A report states that the Old Lifeboat House may be haunted, a toy wholesaler leased it for a while and overnight some of the stock was moved about on the top floor, this happened on several occasions although no actual ghost has been seen.

THE TRAGIC STORY OF JUNE ———

This is a true story — as the pundits say — "the truth is stranger than fiction" and this story is no exception, as one will find.

As this story is based upon actual happenings in Clacton, it is possible that some relatives may still live in the area, therefore, the surnames have been deleted to avoid any possible embarrassment.

This story starts in the summer of 1942 in wartime Clacton, the threat of invasion was never far away, and as with all East Coastal towns — Clacton was mainly occupied by troops. Its beaches were covered with masses of steel scaffolding, coil after coil of barbed wire and beneath the sands — thousands of land mines just waiting for the enemy to put an unwary boot on one.

In 1940, most of the civilian population had been evacuated, especially the children and there was hardly a child to be found anywhere in the Clacton area. But by 1942 a few families had managed to return, much against the Governments advice and wishes, the danger was still very real and great.

It was into these dangerous conditions that two Clacton families returned with their respective daughters June and Christine, both about 14 years of age.

The summer of 1942 was one of the hottest on record at the time. The troops, with very little to do other than watch and wait for the enemy that was expected any day, any night, found themselves with time on their hands. The officers, realising that they had to do something to relieve the tension of their men, allowed a small area near the pier to be cleared of mines and the troops to go in swimming, which of course was greatly appreciated by all.

Children, being children, June and Christine soon made friends with the troops, and it did not take long for them to persuade the officer in charge to allow them to go in swimming as well.

All went well for some weeks, until one fateful day the two girls went down to the beach as usual, they played around with the troops, went in swimming, came out, played around again, thoroughly enjoying themselves. June decided to go in for another swim by herself, the tide was well on its way out and she had to walk almost beyond the pier before the water was deep enough to swim in. When conditions are like that, there are very dangerous undercurrents beyond the pier, and nobody realised that June had reached this dangerous area until it was too late, she was caught in these dreadful currents and not being a strong enough swimmer, was sucked under and carried away before anyone could reach her.

Five days later, her body was washed up on the beach at Holland-on-Sea, opposite the Eastcliff Hotel, some two miles away from where she disappeared.

****

One Sunday evening, some time after the tragedy, the two mothers went to the local Spiritualist Church, a visiting Medium who had no knowledge of the drowning, told June's mother that her daughter would be attending the wedding of her friends daughter when she got married, but this would be some time in the future.

June's mother, being a very experienced Medium herself, did not reject this message out of hand, although she thought to herself, June was drowned about five years earlier, how could she possibly be at Christine's wedding?

A further two years passed and the Medium's message was forgotten about, until one day, another visiting Medium gave an almost identical megsage and about a year later a third Medium repeated the same message. This was all too much of a coincidence, these messages were discussed between the two families many, many times, but at this stage there was no sign of Christine getting married.

However, in 1954, Christine finally agreed to get married, of course the prediction was remembered and everyone concerned speculated as to what might happen and in what form.

The wedding day arrived, it was a fine sunny Saturday, the ceremony was to take place at the Baptist Church in Pier Avenue, Clacton. A crowd had assembled outside the Church waiting for the bride to arrive. At last the car with Christine and her bridesmaids and mother drew up at the kerb side, the driver jumped smartly out and came round to open the rear door for the bride to step out.

Just as the happy Christine was stepping from the car, she appeared to stumble and was prevented from falling by the timely action of the driver. When she recovered her posture the cameras clicked and she, smiling, carried on as if nothing had happened. The ceremony went ahead without any further incident and the very happy bride and groom emerged from the Church to pose for photographs.

Whilst the reception was taking place the photographer returned to his shop to hastily develop his films and return with the prints. The prints were duly pinned upon a board for all to see.

When the guests viewed the photos they were amazed at what they saw on the first that was taken of Christine leaving the car, there, clearly for all to see, on the front of her wedding dress was an imprint of a girls face with a rubber bathing cap on her head, the shape of the face was the same as that of June, the friend that was so tragically drowned some twelve years earlier — the predictions had indeed been proved to be correct.

The photographer, very bewildered by what his work appeared to reveal, hastily returned to his shop to examine the negative and make another print, but with the same result.

A week later, a guest had his film developed and sure enough, there was the face, just as clear as before. Two cameras could not have made the same mistake, the photos must have been taken seconds apart.

But this was not the only surprise that the photographs revealed, upon closer examination, another smaller face was visible on the brides right arm, this was identified as June's grandmother who had been very attached to June and had died shortly after the drowning.

Another strange thing was the appearance of June's initials in one of the 'horseshoes' on her wedding dress, also the brides right hand — it was not the hand of the bride, she has short squat fingers, whereas the photo shows long thin fingers. Could they be those of the grandmother?

As if that was not enough of a story, further information has come to light that has quite a connection with the above story.

CHRISTINE'S WEDDING 1954

1. Grandmothers face in horseshoe.
   Junes initials (J.L.) also in horseshoe.
2. Centre — girls face in swimming hat.
3. Grandmothers hands.

Going back to 1945, Christine's mother was staying the night with June's mother, and was sleeping in the middle bedroom that had been June's room before the tragedy. June's mother was having a restless night, maybe it was because she was in a strange bed, but she just could not sleep, she twisted and turned and laid awake just looking at the shadows around the room.

Between one and two o'clock in the morning, she was suddenly aware of a ghostly figure dressed in a skirt and blouse with a shawl over its shoulders gliding slowly from the closed bedroom door towards the wardrobe. The closed wardrobe door somehow slowly swung open, revealing a rail full of girls clothes, the figure rummaged through them as if searching for some particular item.

She could hardly believe her eyes, in fact she thought that she was having a nightmare, but then she realised who the figure was — it was June's grandmother; they had met briefly once before, that was of course before she died — just over a year earlier, and here she was, back in her dead granddaughters bedroom looking as real as ever.

Clearing her throat, Christine's mother said "Hello, what are you looking for ?" At this the figure turned and disappeared.

Sleep for the rest of the night was even more out of the question, she just laid there waiting for the dawn to come, but in that time the ghostly figure returned twice more, each time searching the wardrobe without success, then gliding back to the door passing through it as if it did not exist!!!

THE HAUNTED SWEET SHOP

About 25 years ago there was a sweet shop in Clacton that was the scene of several unusual and unaccountable happenings.

To say that it was haunted, would not fully describe the strange occurrences there.

One summer evening, as he was in the habit of doing, the owner went back to the shop to re-stock the shelves. He had been working for about half an hour when he suddenly realised that although it was a warm night, the temperature in the shop had fallen. Then without warning a figure parted the bead curtains that divided the stock room from the shop.

This figure appeared to be as solid as a normal human being, but the shopkeeper immediately recognised it to be that of his father who had in fact died about three years earlier. But here he was, dressed in his usual suit, holding the bead curtains apart, looking just the same as he did in life.

The shopkeeper could hardly believe his eyes, he just stood rooted to the spot, he did not feel frightened — just shocked, but a greater shock was yet to come; his father spoke to him "Don't be frightened son, it is me, I have come back to help you." Strangely, as the figure let go the bead curtains they just fell into place without any wavering that one expects from this type of curtain.

It was quite a while before the shopkeeper could stammer out a reply.

This was just the first of many visitations that he had from his father in the following months; if anyone had heard them talking to each other, but could only see the shopkeeper, they would certainly have thought him 'strange' to say the least, perhaps mad. In fact he even had his own doubts to his sanity, and even went so far as to see his doctor over the matter.

Apart from the regular visitations to the shopkeeper, the figure also appeared to the shopkeeper's wife whilst she was working in the shop, he conversed with her as well.

Several strange things also happened in the shop, such as the time when all the plastic 4lb jars became depressed one night, just as if the air had been sucked out and had left a vacuum.

Many times the two electric tills which had been emptied and switched off overnight, were found the next morning plugged in and on each display panel were a line of 7's. After this happened a few times it was reported to the suppliers and in due course the service engineer checked the tills but could not find any faults, he even stated that it was impossible to for a line of sevens to show up on the panel unless the 7 key was repeatedly depressed. However, even after the service, the same thing happened time and time again.

Just in case someone had keys to the doors, the shopkeeper even had all the locks changed, but the mystery of the tills still continued.

It had always been the custom each morning to fill the electric kettle and brew a pot of tea before opening the shop for business — but after the first appearance of his father's ghost, many mornings he would find the kettle filled, plugged in and the kettle hot but switched off!!!

There was the occasion when a relation paid a visit to the shop and whilst talking to the shopkeeper's wife he casually helped himself to a sweet, but before he could put it in his mouth something sharply hit his arm causing the sweet to drop back into the box.

That night the father manifested to his son and remarked that he was watching the relation when he took the sweet and it was he that hit the man's arm, after all, it was the profits that he would have been eating, and how many times had he told his son that he had come back to help him and look after his interests!!

When the father died, he left several very good suits that he'd hardly worn. Rather than give them away to strangers, his widow gave them to a relative who never really got on with her husband.

One night when the apparition manifested to his son, he said that he was furious over his widow giving THAT man his suits, and he would see that they were never worn by him.

Some time later, his widow received a letter from the relatives wife thanking her for the suits, but said that her husband was unable to wear them because when unpacked they were all green with mould!!!

Later, when the shop was eventually sold, strange things still occurred there, but not on the scale as before which suggests that the ghost of the father left with the family.

GREAT CLACTON
UNEXPLAINED FORCES

Over the years there have been several reported cases of people encountering what can only be described as an invisible force.

So far, nobody has been able to arrive at any logical conclusion as to what it is or why it should occur. The only thing that it can be likened to is an invisible barrier.

In Clacton, until a few years ago, there was a row of thatched cottages on the corner of Burrs Road and Valley Road. At the time they were said to have been the oldest remaining dwellings in Great Clacton, but unfortunately, they have now been demolished and the site re-developed.

Just before they were demolished, one of the tenants had a very frightening experience. She was sitting in a rocking chair in her front room with a little child in her arms, gently rocking backwards and forwards and softly singing to the child, when, without any warning, the chair slowly began to rise from the floor until her head was only a few inches from the ceiling. The chair continued the gentle rocking motion despite the fact that it was suspended in mid air with no means of visible support.

Screaming with fright and holding the child tightly in her arms the woman jumped from the moving chair and ran towards the kitchen, but, to her horror, she was unable to reach the door. She found herself pushing against what she later described as an invisible barrier being unable to pass through it, or to go round it and getting more frantic by the second, she turned around and made for the front door, which she reached without any further trouble. Opening it, she ran screaming into the road and headed for her neighbours house.

The neighbour, having quietened the poor woman down and stopping the child from crying, managed to extract the story from her. Picking up a heavy walking stick, he gingerly went around to her house and peered through the still open front door. As far as he could see everything was normal, the rocking chair was back on the floor and nothing seemed disturbed. Cautiously he went into the room, pushing out his stick in front of him, he made for the kitchen door, once again everything was in order, there was just nothing to suggest that anything untoward had ever happened!!

****

THE HAUNTED COTTAGES

There used to be three cottages in Valley Road, Gt. Clacton, near to where the junction of Oxford Road is now. A few years ago these cottages were pulled down to be replaced with modern bungalows.

For many years before the cottages were demolished, one of them was occupied by a lady who claimed to have an unusual type of haunting, whenever she looked into a mirror she saw faces of people standing behind her whom she did not recognise. At first she was rather scared by them, but as time went by she got used to seeing them and even tried to hold a one sided conversation with them.

At the beginning, (just after the 1939/45 war) the faces were seen in her dressing table mirrors only, then she began to see them in her hand mirror and from there on, in every mirror in the house. They were not particularly intimidating faces, but watched every movement that she made with great interest.

There seemed to be no reason as to why this should happen in this cottage or even to this lady, although she certainly did appear to have more than average psychic ability.

THE ROOM WITH A VIEW

Until sometime in the 1960's, what is now St. Johns Road, Great Clacton, was known as St. Osyth Main Road.

About two hundred yards from the centre of the village along this road there was an old public house called The West End Tavern, the landlord was a Mr Rampling. It had been in the Rampling family for many, many, years, until finally the landlord retired and the old Tavern closed down, eventually to be pulled down to make way for the new road which is now called Ramplings Road in memory of the Rampling family.

However, one night, the last Mr Rampling was asleep in his bedroom which overlooked the main road, when he was awakened by a strange noise which appeared to come from the road outside, at first he tried to work out just what the noise was, but could not identify it, so getting out of bed and crossing to the window he was amazed to see two figures in monks habits coming along the road from the direction of the village, it being brilliant moonlight there was no question of making any mistake — they were definitely monks, when they were nearly opposite the pub they crossed the road and disappeared into the very old house nearly opposite, known as the Yew Trees (still in existence). It then struck Mr Rampling that they were not human beings, but two ghosts.

It was some minutes later, when he had fully recovered from the shock of what he had seen, that he realised that the strange sound that had woken him up, was a gentle musical buzzing which increased in volume as the figures approached the inn and decreased as they passed, finally to stop when the figures disappeared into the house.

There have been reports of ghostly monks being seen in and around the Gt. Clacton area, but not along this stretch of road.

THE SHIP INN

Great Clacton's old Ship Inn has seen many changes over the years, in fact it is one of Gt Clacton's oldest public houses, dating back to the time when a fair used to be regularly held on the green in front of it.

There are stories about the tunnels that used to run from its cellars, across the road to the churchyard, also to connect up with its neighbouring house — Eaglehurst.

It is believed that these tunnels were used by smugglers, smuggling of course was very much a way of life in Gt Clacton in days gone by.

As with most old inns, there have been associated stories of ghosts and hauntings, the Ship Inn no doubt also had its share of un-licenced spirits in the past. However, in the 1990's there was one occasion when a barmaid was startled when a Coca Cola advertisement that stood on a shelf in the Public Bar, suddenly crashed to the floor. It had been untouched on that shelf for some length of time and in front of it there was a line of spare glasses and spirit measures, which strangely remained untouched, therefore the sign must have literally jumped over them before crashing to the floor!!

The present landlady has often felt a 'presence' and also feels that she is being watched by some unseen person. But what she found more startling was the time when she was serving a lady in the bar and was asked if she had found the oval mirror yet. When she replied that she knew nothing about such a mirror, the lady answered "you will"!

Some weeks later, when helping her husband to clear out some attic rooms in the inn, there in a cupboard was a large oval mirror !! She is now wondering just what the significance of this mirror is ! Maybe it will reveal some of the Ship's murky past! Who knows — Time alone will tell!!

TREASURE HOLT

A photograph taken of Treasure Holt in the 1930's

Treasure Holt, for many years has held the reputation of being the most haunted house in the district, possibly not without some justification. In the 1920's it was investigated by the Society of Psychical Research. In 1928, a brick floor was being re-laid when some human bones, leather buckles and a token dated 1793, was discovered. In 1972, the B.B.C. Look East Television did a broadcast from there in their Haunted East Anglian Houses series. Numerous newspaper articles have been written about it — and of course, rumours by the score.

However, Treasure Holt as it is known nowadays dates back beyond 1138. In earlier days it was called Perles, or Pearls Farm and there are tales of it even being an Inn at some time in the distant past. But that is another story.

Treasure Holt, even today stands isolated at the far end of the Burrs Estate, set back from the road and one could easily pass by it without knowing it was there.

If all the tales about it were to be believed, it would be absolutely steeped in history, maybe it is!!

But for the purpose of this book we will try to keep to the more plausible tales. (???)

To say that the place is haunted seems to be a gross understatement, even if a past owner whose family lived in the house for over seventy years is to be believed. He related to the writer just a few of his own experiences there — such as the time when he was laying in bed one Sunday morning when he heard a rustling sound, thinking that it was his mother entering the room he did not take too much notice, but as the rustling seemed to cross the floor he looked up, to his utter amazement — he saw a lady dressed in a crinoline gown just about to pass through the door. His mother also saw a lady similarly dressed crossing their lounge about a year later and the figure just faded before her eyes.

Both mother and son also claimed to have seen the apparition of a Cavalier in their lounge, but at different times, and the son said that he once saw Cavaliers and Roundheads having a sword fight on the edge of the lawn in front of the house.

Then there was the time — Boxing Day 1960, when the mother and son with a friend were sitting around the fire at the end of the lounge, when the son saw his deceased father appear through the front wall, dressed in his best suit, the figure then slowly walked to the centre of the room, stopped, turned around, took a long look at the three people, turned again and disappeared through the wall at the far end of the room at a spot where many years ago there used to be a doorway.

The father had died four years earlier — in Ipswich hospital, but the strange thing about it was, the son was the only one who actually saw the apparition!!

Many people claim to have seen a monk in the grounds, usually walking about a foot or so above the ground level as if the ground had sunk but he still walked on the level of the old path.

At various times there have been reports of strange occurrences at or nearby Treasure Holt, such as the time when some people were talking outside the house one day, when they heard sounds of music coming from inside, thinking that this was strange, they looked through the window and saw a lady with long blonde hair seated near the fireplace playing a spinet, but when they opened the door there was nothing to be seen nor heard!!!

Another time, a family were out for a walk one afternoon along the lane which passes by Treasure Holt when they saw a lady with long blonde hair riding a white horse coming towards them, so they moved over to the other side of the road to let them pass, on turning around to look again they found that both horse and rider had completely disappeared near the entrance of the house, although there was a clear view all round there was no sign of either horse or rider.

One wonders if the lady on the white horse was the same lady playing the spinet!!! Also, could the lady on the horse be the same apparition as the one that has often been seen in Pork Lane, Gt. Holland, crossing the road and then riding across the fields in the direction of Treasure Holt?

In the 1980's, the owner at the time, was carrying out some alterations to a chimney, when to his amazement he found two Cromwellian period swords hidden on a ledge inside the chimney itself. Perhaps this might help to give credence to the Cavalier — Roundhead story!!!

THE GHOSTLY MONK

In 1966 a lady who lived in Burrs Road, Clacton, stated that she had seen the figure of a monk dressed in a black cloak with a hood, and that he was very tall, this figure had also been seen on two other occasions by her husband and eldest son, these sightings were just before, and just after Christmas 1964.

The family had lived in this house since it was built some six years prior to the first incident.

The first occasion the figure was seen by her husband who worked on a local farm, was about four o'clock one morning, when shortly after getting up for work, the figure appeared to stand in the doorway, and then disappeared through a ground floor window.

The first occasion that the lady saw the figure, was again about four o'clock in the morning, when she was lying in bed suffering from toothache. She was suddenly aware of someone else in the bedroom and looking up, saw the figure of a monk leaning over her. She immediately screamed for her husband, and the figure disappeared, but she was convinced that this was the same figure previously seen by her husband.

On other occasions she has been conscious of somebody being present in the house, although she could see nothing.

There was the time when her husband was on his way to work early one morning, when he was joined by their son and dog. They had not gone very far along the road, when the dog suddenly stopped and started to bark, its back hair stood up, and the barking turned to a vicious growling, but there was nothing to be seen that could have accounted for its behaviour.

In January 1990, the writer again contacted the lady, who was still living in the same house, but she said that since the earlier mentioned occurrences, she was not aware of anything else happening.

However, between the twenty-four years spanning the two interviews, other people had seen a figure of a tall monk, slightly stooped, walking along the nearby lanes but, in these cases the monk had appeared to have been walking some inches above the surface of the ground, as if he had been walking along some ancient path and the ground had sunk beneath it.

The old farmhouse of Treasure Holt is only some 250 yards away, so it is quite possible that the ghostly monks reported to have been seen there, are the same as those seen at this house and along the road.

However, researches revealed that many years ago there was an Order of monks in a monastery at St. Osyth; also there was a small church close to Little Holland Hall. This church was serviced at the time by monks from St. Osyth, who used to walk along the lanes and footpaths, through the forest as it was in those days, to and from the little church that was on the cliff top. Also that there is a distinct possibility that in days gone by, there could have been an earlier dwelling built on the site of the lady's house, and the monks just possibly could have been in the habit of calling at this dwelling for some refreshment, or even to attend a sick occupier, the path between the monastery and the church could well have taken them past the house, and the four o'clock in the morning sightings could well be about the correct timing to arrive in time for the early services.

****

OUT OF TOWN STORIES

THE SQUIRES BED

At Gallows Corner, near Gidea Park, Romford, the gibbet was taken down in the eighteenth century. The local squire claimed the wood and promptly had it made into a four poster bed.

When the village carpenter erected it in the squires bedroom, the squire tested it and jokingly said "I shall sleep the sleep of the dead tonight." The next morning he was found dead in the bed!!!

THE HAUNTED RESTAURANT

In Gt. Clacton there was a restaurant in one of the holiday camps that had a little old lady dressed in black for a ghost. She appeared several times over the years and seems to have favoured Easter Monday for her regular visits, although she had been known to show herself at other times.

One of these 'other times', was when the restaurant had a Spanish chef who was well known to like to have a bottle of wine in the kitchen for his own personal use. One day he was having a swig at the bottle, when he was suddenly aware of a figure of a little old lady standing in the doorway shaking her head. Not knowing the story of the haunting, he turned and started to tell her that customers were not allowed into his kitchen, at the same time walking towards her still with the bottle in his hand. When he was about two paces from her she just disappeared and he was so startled that he dropped the bottle swearing that he would never drink again whilst working and believe it or not, he didn't touch another bottle for the rest of that season.

Then there was the time, when one Easter Monday, a young waitress who had only worked at the restaurant for a few days saw a little old lady dressed all in black sitting at one of her tables. Again not knowing anything about the hauntings, she went up to the lady and started to apologise for keeping her waiting, explaining that she did not see her come in. The old lady looked at her, smiled, then disappeared. The waitress was so shocked that she left the restaurant immediately and did not even go back for the wages that were due to her.

Sometime later a seance was held in the restaurant. The psychic medium was not told where the seance was being held nor given any indication as to why the seance was being held at this particular place; she was collected from her house by a taxi, blindfolded, then driven by a roundabout route to the restaurant.

Once seated, the medium was soon able to make contact with the spirit of a little old lady whom she described exactly as every reported sighting had described her. When asked as to why she kept returning to the restaurant, the lady replied that she used to live here with her husband who was a farmer, but when he died she was swindled out of the property by some estate agents, and was forced to live in poverty until she died, and that she was not very happy about it and was biding her time until she could get the property back.

The medium explained to her that she was now dead, and would not have any need to have the place back anyway, also the old farmhouse as she would have known it, had been pulled down some years ago, and a new building had been built on the spot.

Because of her obvious unhappiness at the situation as she saw it, she remained earthbound, but the medium was certain that if only she could come to terms with the situation, she would be able to pass on to a better world and the material things of this world would no longer trouble her.

A check back a couple of years after the seance, revealed that the apparition of the 'little old lady' had only been seen once since, when she appeared to be smiling, then she waved, as if to say "Good Bye" and faded away..

THE APPARITIONS IN THE FLAT

There is a flat in the centre of Gt. Clacton over a shop which surely must rate as one of the oldest buildings left in the village.

The occupier related just a few of the things that she had seen, heard, and experienced in the four years that she had lived there, some of them defied explanation.

In 1987, just two days after the great gale had struck this area, she was in one of the bedrooms of the flat, when she saw the figure of a man standing in the doorway, he was dressed in what could have been 16th century clothes, or possibly old clerical attire.

He wore a tall black hat, that had a small rim, with a shiny black band around it, a buckle or similar type badge in the front. He had a dark, Spanish type complexion and a large nose, long shoulder length hair, a white frilly ruff around his neck that had a white frilly piece to the front. He was wearing a black fitted jacket that was pulled in at the waist, his trousers were more like pantaloons that ended just below his knees, with long stockings from his knees to his feet, his shoes were buckled, the buckles were similar to the one on his hat. He stood there for what seemed ages, but was in fact only a few moments, before he turned and disappeared.

There is a winding staircase that goes from the lounge to a large attic room which goes the full length of the building. It was in this attic room that she has also heard children talking and playing, yet when she has looked up there, there was nothing to be seen. During the war years, this room was used as billets for the troops, and for years since, there was a list of the occupants fixed behind the door, recently this has just disappeared without trace.

Items have disappeared, only to reappear in other places at later dates. In the kitchen, the refrigerator door has several little magnetic figures on it, over night, or when there is nobody at home, these figures somehow leave the fridge door and can be found attached to any metal object, even stuck to the metal bowl of the sink unit.

At the bottom of the stairs there is an area where the temperature seems to drop considerably at odd times, and visitors have often remarked that they 'feel a nasty presence' when they pass this spot.

THE PHANTOM HORSE

Until the 1950's, there used to be a large house at Gt. Clacton called Smoaky House, situated near to the roundabout at the junction of London Road and St. John's Road.

Rumours of the old house being haunted have abounded for years, but curiously, no one seems to remember what it was supposed to be haunted by. But not so on the piece of land by the corner of the roundabout, where there used to be a large black weatherboarded barn which was eventually pulled down in the 1960's.

It is said that many times before the 1939/45 war, a riderless phantom horse had been seen to cross the roundabout and to disappear into this barn. Since the war, however, there have only been a few reports of the horse having been seen, and none since the old barn was pulled down. Whether there is actually any connection between the demolition of the barn and the lack of sightings is doubtful, but more likely, with the increase of modern traffic creating unfavourable conditions the horse does not manifest itself. But it would be interesting to hear if the ghostly mare should appear again!!

****

OUT OF TOWN STORIES

THE CHURCHYARD WATCHERS

In olden days it was often the custom to have what was believed to be certain people buried whose 'after life' job was to see over the graves of others, these were known as the 'Churchyard Watchers.'

At Little Ilford there are records of a number of servants being buried outside the church grounds in order that their spirits should protect the graves of their former employers!!

THE PLOUGH INN MYSTERIES

The old Plough Inn at Great Clacton dates back many years, although possibly not the oldest 'refreshment house' in the village, it is by far the smallest — and for some reason it appears to have the most unsolved mysteries attached to it.

Although many strange unaccountable things have happened here over the years, it is only this last few years that notes have been made at the time of the 'happenings'. To mention but a few, we have the time when a previous landlady had her hand on a downstairs door handle when she felt a very strong male hand being placed over hers, thinking it was her husbands, she looked round, but started screaming when she realised that there was nobody there — the pressure on her hand stopped as soon as she screamed.

Then there was the time when the same landlord and his wife were in the bar waiting to open up, when they heard something running along the upstairs passageway, thinking that it was their dogs chasing the cat, they weren't too bothered, but when the same thing happened again a few minutes later — enough was enough. The husband went upstairs to sort the animals out, but to his amazement, not only were both dogs asleep in their baskets, a search revealed that the cat was out. There was nothing visible to account for the noise which apparently the dogs did not hear.

Another night, after closing time, one of the dogs was sitting on a chair in the bar with its ears pricked up staring intensely at a chair in the corner, just as if it was looking at something or someone.

Even more recently, when the landlord and his family were on holiday and a temporary manager was in charge. It was a Sunday morning about 11.55 a.m. when the manager was making a last minute check around before opening at 12 o'clock — the handle of the bar door started rattling as if a customer was impatient to get in, the dog ran to the door barking — the manager looked through the window towards the door, but could see no one, holding the still barking dog, he unlocked the door and cautiously opened it, but apart from a gentleman sitting in a car outside, the street was clear. He asked the motorist if he had been to the door, shaking his head, he said that he hadn't, and there had not been anyone near the Inn for some minutes!!!

Although in all these cases nothing was actually seen, many times people have felt that there is someone watching and waiting — but what for???

THE SURPRISE IN THE GARDEN

There is a certain business in the centre of Gt. Clacton where, although their family have owned the premises for many years, have never seen anything in the house that suggests that it is haunted, although for a long time — quite a few years, in fact, they have been aware of a 'presence'. Many are the times when they have turned to see who is approaching them from behind, but every time it is the same answer — No one.

There have been numerous occasions when there has been a strong aroma of violets wafting through the house, always the same smell, but despite every attempt to locate its source, nothing as yet has been found to account for it.

Although no apparitions have manifested inside the house, what has been seen in the garden is a different story — . There was the time when the present owner was down the garden picking some stick runner beans, when he thought that he saw something move between the rows, thinking that it was one of the children playing games, he carried on picking the beans — when all of a sudden he saw the figure of his father standing before him — it was so solid and real, he just could not believe it, after all, his father had been dead for some years!

By the time that he had regained his senses, the figure had faded away, still leaving him with the question — why should his father suddenly appear, he wasn't even thinking about him at the time and he hadn't appeared before, so why should he now??

Whenever the owner went down the garden after that incident, he found a wonderful feeling of tranquillity, a feeling that he had never experienced there before!!

****

A DEFINITION

There is a very apt definition of superstition — mental depravity arising from ignorance.

THE SWINGING HIGHWAYMAN

Legend has it that many years ago a local highwayman was not content with holding up travellers passing through the district, he started to rob the local people as well.

The villagers got so fed up with his antics, that one day a group of them went to see him, and warned him to leave the villagers alone and stick to robbing strangers. He laughed at them and remarked that not one of them was man enough to come and tell him on their own, they had to gang up on him.

He still continued to rob and pillage the locals as before, until one dark night a group of men ambushed him and hanged him from a tree on the corner of Burrs road. His body was left swinging from an old oak, not only as a warning to others, but to show the villager's triumph over one who had terrorised them for so long.

It is said that at times his ghostly figure could be seen swinging to and fro in the wind, until just before the last war when the tree was cut down.

LITTLE CLACTON

THE HAUNTED CHURCHYARD

There have always been stories of haunted churchyards, and children have been known to cross the road rather than pass too close to a graveyard. This strange conduct is not always restricted to children either. Even the hardiest of adults have been known to shudder and refuse to cross a churchyard at night. In the days when the village policeman used to ride around his beat on a bicycle and was on night duty, if he was truthful, he would admit that the last place he would want to be at midnight would be near the churchyard.

This is a phenomenon that has been instilled in us almost since birth, but why ? In this enlightened day and age, common sense should tell us that there is nothing to fear ———.

However, Little Clacton's churchyard is reputed to have had a ghost for just 400 years, and certainly not one to be afraid of — it is said to be the apparition of Prudence Lambert who took her own life way back in 1592.

On Tuesday, 15th August 1592, Prudence Lambert was married to Nicholas Lambert of Clacton Lodge, but by the next morning she had hung herself.

Because she had taken her own life, according to custom, she was buried on the north side of the Little Clacton church in unconsecrated ground.

Since then, her ghost is said to haunt the old wooden shed to the north of the graveyard. It is also said that not only does Prudence haunt the churchyard, but her spirit also returns to Clacton Lodge!!

THE HOLLAND ROAD FIGURES

One freezing, snowy February night about 2 a.m., a young man was called from his home in Thorpe-le-Soken to his father's house in Clacton where a water pipe had burst and was flooding the place.

As it was freezing hard and the roads were treacherous, he was only able to drive slowly.

Travelling from Thorpe via Tan Lane, he turned left into Holland Road, and was astonished to see a man walking on the near side of the road. Although he was travelling at a very low speed, road conditions were such that he dare not touch his brakes or make any sharp turn to avoid the man. In fact, he half expected to feel a slight bump on the side of the car indicating that he had actually hit him.

However, there was no bump, and when he looked round there was nobody to be seen!!

The figure was that of an elderly man, of heavy build and medium height, but what was more startling was his clothes; he was dressed in a three quarter length coat and a tall 'chimney pot' hat, typical of Victorian times. Although his features were not distinct, he certainly had a pointed beard. In his hand he held a stick which appeared to have a knob for a handle, and he was holding this stick in front of him using it with a prodding motion as if he were blind.

The driver said, that although he did not actually see it, he had the impression that the old man was wearing a waistcoat with a gold watch chain across the front of his stomach!!

This all happened in the mid 1980's.

Other people have reported seeing a similar figure which has sometimes been accompanied by a female who is usually hooded.

A hooded female has also been seen walking in the rear garden of a nearby cottage.

Just who this couple were still remains a mystery, but maybe one day the answer will be found, also the reason for their occasional manifestations.

THE LAUGHING POLICEMAN

When a family moved to an old house in Holland Road, Little Clacton, they thought that they had left a family ghost behind them, but it appears that when they moved, the ghost moved with them.

There were two young boys in the family and as boys will, they argued over each others toys. But the parents thought that they had found the perfect answer to the problem when they gave each boy a cupboard that could be locked to keep their toys in.

Peace ruled for some time, until one boy was given a battery operated 'Laughing Policeman'. Both boys liked playing with the toy, but many a time they nearly came to blows over it, so the parents insisted that it was locked away.

One day, whilst the boy whose toy it was, was away, and the other boy was playing in their bedroom, the 'Laughing Policeman' started to laugh.

The boy's mother heard the laughter and called out to the lad in the bedroom to put his brother's toy away. When the boy came into the lounge, his mother told him that he was not to touch his brother's toys when he was not there, in any case he should not have unlocked his brother's cupboard. The boy denied unlocking the cupboard, let alone playing with that toy. At this moment the laughter was heard again, this time there was nobody upstairs.

When their father came in and was told what had happened, he went to the cupboard, unlocked it and took the toy out, to everyone's surprise — there were no batteries in it!!!

ST. OSYTH

THE LEGEND OF ST. OSYTH

After the nunnery had been established for some time it was raided by a band of Vikings led by Inguar and Hubba who landed on the nearby coast. After plundering the village they turned their attention to the nunnery, after raping and killing some of the nuns they seized Osyth and took her into what is now known as Nun's Wood and tried to get her to renounce her religion, when she flatly refused to do this, they forced her head forward and with one blow of a sword decapitated her and her head fell to the ground.

Legend has it, that the Danes were amazed when the headless body bent down and with her hands picked up her head, holding it at arms length, and with slow steady steps the headless body walked across the fields back to the village, led by an angel to the Church of St. Peter and St. Paul, where finding the door locked, knocked on the door with her bloodstained hands, leaving traces of blood on the door and then she fell to the ground.

Another legend has it that on the spot where Osyth's head fell after the decapitation, a fountain of pure water gushed up and was used as a cure for many diseases.

For many years a legend has been believed that every October 7th. the ghost of Osyth can be seen at midnight walking the short distance from Nun's Wood to the church with her headless body holding her head in her outstretched hands.

Over the years, literally thousands of people have gathered in all weathers, near the church at midnight on October 7th. hoping to catch a glimpse of Osyth's ghost!!!

MORE ST. OSYTH HAUNTINGS

One night a lady who lived in one of the houses in The Bury, at St. Osyth, found that she was being prevented from entering her own gateway by "a very big black dog that barred her way and then suddenly vanished".

At first her husband thought that this might have been an appearance of "Black Shuck", the legendary black hound that is reputed to haunt some coastal areas. However, when telling neighbours of his wife's experience, it was revealed that a previous tenant of the house once had such a dog, which had been run over and killed on the road outside the house and it's apparition had been seen before.

****

One night a St. Osyth man was passing by the Priory side gate, when he was suddenly aware of something following him. Looking round, he saw the shape of a small creature, too small to have been a man or even a child, but it was definately a biped. He stopped walking and turned around to face whatever it was, — as he turned he saw the figure slowly disintegrate in front of him!!

****

The area around The Goodlife Public House, Spring Road, St Osyth, also has a reputation for being haunted.

One apparition is said to walk across the road near the pub dressed in a Bomber Jacket and Jeans. It is thought to be a boy about 14/15 years of age and when seen appears to be quite solid.

And the phantom of a boy is also said to have been seen around the Goodlife Stables. Perhaps this is the same boy?

There does not appear to be any reason for these apparitions to appear here, there are no records of any tragedy occurring involving a boy of this age, so perhaps it is just one of after-life's mysteries and as they say — "All will be revealed one day".

THORPE-LE-SOKEN

THE HAUNTED BELL INN

This old Inn was once the Church House and was occupied in the middle 1740's by Rev Alexander Henry Gough B.A. the vicar of Thorpe-le-Soken and his wife Catherine, commonly known as Kitty.

There is quite a story about Kitty's exploits, but as they say — "That is another story".

The Bell Inn, as it is called nowadays, has created its own story over the years, some parts of it can be associated with Kitty, other parts —-. Well, — who knows when the supernatural takes a hand in affairs.

Over the years many people have reported unaccountable and strange 'happenings' at The Bell, most of which have been accredited to Kitty Canham's ghost returning to try to make amends for the way she treated her husband.

Strangely, there have been only a few reports of a ghost actually being seen or heard there, mainly feelings and results of poltergeist activity.

Bedroom No 6, seems to be where most of the action takes place —. In August 1972, a male guest spending the night in this room, woke the next morning to find that the heavy oak wardrobe had moved across the room, the bedclothes on a spare bed had been disarrayed and the pillow doubled up. The door had been locked from the inside with the key left in the lock, so nobody could have entered the room. Being a very heavy sleeper he had not heard anything being moved and he said that he certainly was not given to sleepwalking.

Room No 8, has also had it share of 'happenings'. A previous owner said that her pet poodle was in the room when it suddenly bared his teeth, raised his hackles and appeared to follow something round the room with it's eyes, after this incident it absolutely refused to enter the room again!

Another time a lady was cleaning some brass in No 8, when she clearly felt a hand clutch at her shoulder, yet there was no one else in the room!

Two guests were shown into the room to stay the night, within a matter of minutes they were back in the bar asking for another room as there was no way they would spend the night in that room!

Another of the bedrooms has a reputation of suddenly turning 'icy cold' and the oppressive feeling of a 'presence' being there. The same feelings can be felt in the corridor outside the bedrooms!!

In November 1974, the B.B.C. Television programme 'On Camera' sent a production team to try to capture Kitty Canham's ghost on film, but despite the efforts of two Spiritualist Mediums they failed to make contact with her.

There is a sequel to the Kitty Canham haunting story -

Many times over the years, it has been reported that villagers of Thorpe making their way home late at night, have been astounded to see an old fashioned horse-drawn funeral cortege slowly making its way along the main road towards the church. One can only assume that this is a re-enactment of Kitty's own funeral!!

THE HAUNTED POLICE STATION

Throughout the country wherever there have been places that people have been held in captivity, whether it be an old village 'cage' or lock up, to a dank, dingy dungeon in some obscure castle, there have always been stories of apparitions appearing at odd times, perhaps that of some poor soul who spent his last few days on this earth incarcerated under terrible conditions with death being his only release.

Not suggesting that Thorpe-le-Soken Police Station was quite as bad as that, nor that anybody had actually died whilst being held in its two cells, but —-, nevertheless there are strange circumstances that have occurred that certainly makes one think twice about wanting to spend a night inside these old cells!

This old Police Station was built around 1850 and today is about the oldest fully operational one in Essex, at one time it was important enough to warrant having a Superintendent in charge, with a Station Sergeant living in the adjoining building.

A part of the building was used as a Magistrates Court and an old 'Cell Book' has survived the ravages of time to reveal some misdemeanours that came before the Bench, — Leaving wife and thirteen children. — One month in Norwich Prison. Stealing growing watercress. — Remanded to Ipswich Prison. Stealing whelks from Brightlingsea. — Committed to Colchester for remand. Being a wandering lunatic. — Three days in the Workhouse. None of these 'crimes' would hardly be bad enough to make a 'spirit' become earthbound, nor want to return to get its revenge. But, it has been known a few times for the old prisoners brass 'call bell' to ring quite loudly, although there were no occupants in the cells at the time!!

There was the time when a Sergeant was on duty one night by himself, the bell rang — giving him quite a fright, pulling himself together, he picked up his truncheon and went cautiously to inspect the two empty cells — all the doors were locked and there was no sign of any intruders, he was just leaving the cell area — when the bell started to ring again, this time he actually saw the bell moving on its spring. This was just too much for him, he ran out of the Station and kept away until daylight!!

Other reports tell of a ghostly police officer being seen, dressed in an old fashioned buttoned up to the neck tunic, with a thick leather belt having the cell keys hanging from it. He was rather short for a policeman of those days and rather stout, with a round jovial face. Some officers on night duty will tell of mysterious voices coming from the cells, sometimes shouting, sometimes just whispers — either way both are pretty scarey at three o'clock in the morning!

THE CHAINED MAN

There is an old cottage near the War Memorial at Thorpe-le-Soken, in fact it is reputed to be the oldest remaining cottage in the village.

There are stories of it being haunted, although the present owners were not aware of anything untoward in the cottage, they always felt that there should be a resident ghost. After all, the whole setting is just right for one, the front door is only about five feet in height and one has to duck to enter the house, the ground floors even had to be lowered to prevent heads being banged on the many oak beams, and there is a beautiful old brick inglenook fireplace, in fact it should be the ideal setting for any well trained ghost.

The story of its haunting was related by a man who actually experienced the manifestation in the bedroom of the cottage when he was a boy.

He used to go to the cottage to play with the boy and girl who lived there. One day the three of them were playing in the bedroom as usual, when they were suddenly aware of the figure of a man standing in the corner of the room, the two children who lived there were not the least afraid of the figure as they had seen it many times before and there was nothing to be frightened of, the man just stood there watching for a while and then disappeared as quickly as he appeared.

One day just after the figure had appeared, the young girl went downstairs and asked her mother "who was the man standing in the bedroom ?" Her mother told her that she must be imagining it, but the girl said that both she and her brother had seen the man many times and so had their friend.

Their mother was even more surprised when the girl then asked "Mummy, why has the man always got chains on his arms and legs ?"

So far the mystery has not been solved, but maybe one day all will be revealed — who knows!!!

THE MYSTERIOUS 'THING'

About the 1930's, a 13 year old school girl and her friend were standing near the War Memorial at Thorpe-le-Soken waiting for a bus one dark evening, when they saw a 'great white round shape' bounding towards them from the direction of Landermere Road.

They were both frozen to the spot and the 'thing' passed right through them and continued bounding along the Walton Road towards Kirby Cross.

There is no record of anything like this having been seen before, it was like a round white cloud — two to three feet in diameter, and there was no feeling of anything 'touching' them when it 'passed through them'.

WEELEY

THE MANOR HOUSE AND IT'S GHOST

When The Manor House at Weeley was offered for sale, a resident ghost was included in the price.

The ghost, thought to be that of an old housekeeper, was found to be a very friendly spirit.

The owners at the time, had lived in the eight-bedroomed old house in The Street for some three years and during that time many strange things were reputed to have happened, nothing really to be scared of — just eerie. Things mysteriously went missing or had been moved without explanation. Old fashioned hairpins appeared in various parts of the house, occupants of some of the bedrooms have felt a 'presence' in their rooms, although they had not been told of it's haunting.

Over the years there have been many sightings by past residents of an old lady, one even claimed that his room had even been tidied up whilst he was out. The owner's wife said that it was more like having a naughty child about the place playing practical jokes and she was never frightened of being alone in the house.

The house had originally been two cottages, but had been made into one large house by the Weeley family, who had been earlier owners for many generations.

Mr Roger Weeley said that it was well known in his family that there were eerie goings-on in the house and related how a whole dinner service had been mysteriously moved from the dresser in the kitchen, cleaned and put back, in fact the whole kitchen had been spring cleaned by the ghostly housekeeper.

HOLLAND-ON-SEA

THE RANDY GHOST

A lady who lived in Aylesbury Drive reported that she has twice been raped by a ghost which attacked her in bed. The next morning there have been large bruises on her thighs, thus proving that it was not a dream. On the last occasion, she struggled out of bed and was amazed to find that the bed was still moving up and down despite the fact that she was standing beside it.

Since the last incident she has taken to wearing a crucifix around her neck at night — there have been no further attacks!

****

There are stories of a perfumed ghost that has been smelt rather than seen along the footpath that runs from the Oakwood Inn towards Aylesbury Drive.

****

THE PHANTOMS OF HOLLAND HAVEN

There have been many reports of 'grey wispy figures' appearing near the site of the ancient burial ground close to Little Holland Hall. Some of these figures are said to appear near the large pond as if searching for something, perhaps these are the apparitions of bygone smugglers still trying to recover some of their contraband that they hid in the pond and failed to recover at the time.

Apart from the old burial ground on this corner of the main road, there are the remains of an old chapel. Records however, reveal that there were never any burials within the grounds of the chapel, so the skeletons that have been found only a couple of feet below ground level in the grounds of the Hall in what appears to be a mass grave, are presumed to be pre-Saxon.

However, there are tales of 'ghostly monks' having been seen in this area, perhaps they had a connection with the old chapel — or possibly with the smugglers!!!

THE MYSTERY AND GHOST OF PORK LANE

There is a farm in Pork Lane, Great Holland, that has a pond which was once said to have been 'bottomless'.

However, this myth was destroyed in 1947, when a severe drought caused the water level to drop considerably.

The farmer thought that this would be an opportune time to not only clean out the pond, (something that had not been done in living memory) but also to solve two other mysteries at the same time — The actual depth of the so called 'bottomless' pond, and the mystery of the 'missing' bull.

Going back to the days when horse power on four legs was the most important item on a farm, and at the end of a long hot day ploughing, the farm hands would bring their tired horses up to the pond and allow them to wander in and have a good drink and no doubt wash away some of the day's dust.

One day, the farm bull which was allowed to wander through the farm yard, stood watching the horses drinking merrily, when suddenly it took it into its head to imitate them and walk into the pond, but the sad story is — it kept on walking until it disappeared below the surface.

The watching farm hands could not believe what they had just seen and when they recovered from the shock, one of them went to find a strong rope, with which they tried dragging the pond to recover the bull, but with no success.

However, the 1947 lack of rain, allowed the remaining water to be pumped out and an amazing collection of accumulated rubbish was revealed and removed — but strangely enough, there was no sign of the bull — no bones, not even its skull!!

What about the 'bottomless' pond ? — Well, at its deepest point it would have been at least fourteen feet deep!!

To this day the 'Mystery of the Bull' remains.

A ghostly horse has been seen many times near the level crossing in Pork Lane, Gt. Holland. Sometimes it is riderless, but other times it appears to be ridden by a young lady with long fair hair. Could this be the same apparition that has been seen near Treasure Holt ? The description is the same and it is no great distance between the two places across the fields!

Also, there is record of a Kate Slough being drowned whilst out riding on her white horse. Both the horse and rider were drowned whist attempting to cross a flooded tributary of Holland Brook. A possible connection??

****

OUT OF TOWN STORIES

THE HEADLESS HEARSE DRIVER

There is an old story from Mistley, where a headless hearse driver has been seen many times driving his horse hearse along The Walls, near Mistley Towers.

Perhaps somebody knows the full story as to how he lost his head. It would be interesting to find out!

WALTON-ON-THE-NAZE

THE SEA CAPTAIN

There is a house in Mill Lane, Walton-on-the-Naze, that has an unusual haunting, it not only has a ghost of a ships Captain, but also a poltergeist. There is a possibility they could be one and the same, although the antics of the latter would hardly be the actions expected of a sea Captain, even a ghostly one.

The apparition of the sea Captain was active from the early 1970's, but whether it had been seen before that date it is not known.

The house in the 1970's was occupied by a Trinity House Pilot, who, because of his duties often had to be called out at odd hours during the night.

One night they had guests staying in the house, and the next morning at breakfast they mentioned that it was a pity that their host was called out during the night. When the hostess asked what made them think that he had been called out, one of them said that he had woken up and in the bright moonlight had clearly seen a figure dressed in naval uniform pass across the bottom of their bed. Thinking that their host had been called out and required something from the wardrobe, he had crept into the bedroom not wishing to disturb his guests.

The hostess apologised for them being disturbed, but explained that her husband had not been called out that night, but they must have seen the ghost of the sea Captain who was reputed to haunt the house.

Some time later, after the same apparition had been seen a few times, they decided to call in a Spiritualist Medium to try to contact the spirit and find out what it was all about.

In due course a Medium held a seance there and made contact with a Captain, who told the small audience that his ship had been wrecked in the Walton Backwater and had lost his life.

Given this information, further research revealed that indeed a ship had been wrecked in the area stated, also the master had gone down with it. His body was later recovered and brought to the beach for removal to the mortuary, but owing to a delay in the body being collected, it was later decided to take the corpse into this house to await collection the next day.

As to why the spirit should wish to return is not known, maybe it felt at peace here?

Regarding the poltergeist, no explanation can be given for such activity.

This mischievous ghost liked to slam doors, move items from one place to another and generally make itself a nuisance, but its party piece was to throw sweets in the air, especially when there were guests in the house.

This would hardly have been the action of a sea Captain, so it is reasonable to assume that there must have been two entities in this house.

OTHER WALTON HAUNTINGS

WALTON HALL

The ruin of the 400 year old Walton Hall with its tower, is said to have been haunted for many years, and when one explores (with great difficulty) its dank, dark cellars, there can be little doubt there could be more than a grain of truth in some of these stories.

Although described as cellars, a more correct description would be 'dungeons', for it is within these dripping walls there are the rotting remains of the old stocks, still enclosed in what was once a 'cage', where prisoners were held until such time as they could be removed to a prison.

In this part of the country, it was more than likely that the prisoners that were held in this 'cage' were not just ordinary villains, but captured smugglers — men who would kill to save their own skins, perhaps some of the ghosts that still haunt the old Walton Hall are the spirits of their victims or maybe those of the smugglers themselves!!

THE TOWER

One could hardly visit Walton without seeing the 81 foot high Tower on the Naze, perched high on the cliff top visible for miles around, in fact that is exactly why it was built in 1720 by the Corporation of Trinity House as a guiding beacon for shipping.

Over the years there have been stories of the Tower being haunted, but the most convincing tale yet, comes from an incident during the 1939/45 war, when it was taken over for military purposes.

Before the days of radar, the main means of keeping a watch for the possible approach of enemy invasion forces, was to have look-outs in high buildings over-looking the sea where they could observe the movements of shipping, and what better place could there have been than the Tower.

However, one day the duty look-out was suddenly seen and heard, running from the tower screaming that he had seen a ghost in the tower.

Of course being wartime, the matter was hushed up, but even so, "Walls had ears" and the locals soon got to hear about it and with a nod and a wink would say "I could have told you so"!!

THE MABEL GRENVILLE HOME

The Mabel Grenville Home, formally known as Highcliffe was designed and built as a mansion in 1880, but was later converted into flats just before the 1939/45 war. The building, built high up on the Walton ciffs had a commanding view of the sea.

During the war most of these flats were occupied by the military, and in a few cases by army families. It was about this time that there was quite a lot of trouble with the families, who complained that the building was haunted, at first the stories were taken lightly, but as time went on and the complaints more frequent, the army authorities realising that there was something going on that they could not deal with began to move the families to other accommodation.

Another story that concerned the house, was that a man, a possible German spy, was caught while signalling out to sea, perhaps to a German U-boat

KIRBY-LE-SOKEN. (LOWER KIRBY)

TALES OF THE RED LION

The old Red Lion Inn at Kirby-le-Soken, dates back to the 1300's, it is even older than the old church opposite, in fact, it is quite possible that some builders of the church even lodged here, and almost certainly sampled some of the ale that was sold, and perhaps some of the brandy and Geneva that was readily available, thanks to local smugglers.

Legend has it, there was a tunnel running from the Red Lion, out beyond its back garden, down to the edge of the Saltings. With smuggling being rife in days gone by, this would have been an ideal spot for them to unload and store their contraband, and of course the inn was the perfect outlet for the selling of it to equally willing buyers.

Rumours tell of a further tunnel extending to the churchyard just across the road. All this ties up with other legends — churches and pubs being linked by tunnels, not only for the use of smugglers, but also as a means of escape for clergy when they were having troubled times, and in this instance, for sixteenth century religious refugees.

Many years ago, when most villages had their own stocks, pillories, possibly a ducking stool and a village 'cage' in which offenders were placed, no doubt Kirby-le-Soken was no exception. The village 'cage' which was in use until the 1860's, was constructed with iron bars and was situated on what used to be a triangular grass 'island' at the junction with Halstead Road. Having served its purpose for many years, it gradually became a rusty eyesore and was removed. Now the only reminder of its very existence is in the name of Cage Corner.

Near to the old 'cage' there used to be the village pillory, but with the course of time, the base of the post rotted and the pillory fell down. However, all was not lost, the remainder of the pillory thankfully was kept and placed in the Red Lion yard for safe keeping, it is complete with the very old padlock still intact. Maybe one day it will be repaired and restored in its original position, and who knows — even put to its original use.

The old Red Lion has a long legend of being haunted, a past occupier told of two phantom children having been seen upstairs in one of the front bedrooms, and a more recent occupant has heard children's voices upstairs and on many occasions heavy footsteps walking across the floor upstairs.

On another occasion the back door latch rattled and the sound of the door opening and partly closing was clearly heard, followed by heavy footsteps crossing the room, going up the stairs and ending in one of the upstairs rooms, but nothing was seen and when the back door was checked it was securely shut!!

There are stories of other 'happenings' in and around the old Inn, which possibly could be connected with the olden days of smuggling. Of course, some of these tales were deliberately spread by the smugglers themselves in order to scare the superstitious villagers away so that they would not see what was going on beyond the Red Lion's back yard!!

****

OUT OF TOWN STORIES

THE VICAR'S SURPRISE

The old Langenhoe church, now demolished, and the nearby manor house were once the scenes of many strange happenings.

From 1937, the hapless vicar experienced a varity of phenomena, apparitions, footsteps, voices, smells, especially of violets.

But the most frightening of all occurred when the poor man was sleeping in the old manor house, he woke to find himself in the cold embrace of a naked female ghost!!

GREAT BENTLEY

GHOSTLY OUTRIDER

Legend has it that years ago at Gt. Bentley a highwayman was about to hold up a stage coach, and the horse bolted and the coach crashed, killing its occupants and possibly the highwayman as well. The only apparent survivor was the outrider.

Occasionally nowadays the apparition of a horseman dressed in old fashioned riding habit, can be seen riding through the country lanes in the Gt. Bentley area.

Could it be that the apparition is the surviving outrider still trying to make amends for failing to protect his charge or could it be the earthbound spirit of the highwayman still paying penance for causing the deaths of the others??

****

Some years ago the remains of a Rhinoceros were found in a field on Dines Farm, Gt. Bentley. It is not suggested that its ghost still roams around the district. But — it was reported that a large unidentified shape was the cause of a car swerving off the road into a ditch one Christmas Eve. Mind you, there are a lot of 'spirits' about at this time of the year.

****

THE ST. ANDREWS ROAD MYSTERY

There is a house in St. Andrews Road, Clacton, that backs on to the site of the old Malvern laundry, where a ghost of a lady dressed in white has often been seen in a bedroom, she then walks through the house opening doors.

The occupier's dog knows when there is something strange about, it growls and backs away from some unseen object and it's hackles rise.

A figure in white has also been seen gliding along a passage between the house and the old laundry, but whether it is the same one is not known.

BRADFIELD

THE SANDEMAN PORT GHOST

Way back in the 1940's, a farm bailiff and his wife managed a farm at Bradfield. One evening they went to a dance at nearby Manningtree. After the dance, they were returning home on their bicycles, being a bright moonlight night, also being wartime, they had to have their front lamps partially blacked out, the resulting light given out was hardly effective.

As they cycled along, they soon came to a farmhouse half way down a hill, the house was partially obscured by a clump of tall trees which stretched from the front of the house down to the roadside.

When nearly level with the farmhouse they became aware of a figure of a tall man standing on the far side of the road just beyond the trees, he was dressed in what could be loosely described as a 'Sandeman Port' outfit — a long black cloak and a tall wide brimmed black hat. He was then joined by a smaller figure also dressed in black, the two figures started to cross the road right in front of the cyclists.

The bailiff being slightly ahead of his wife, managed to swerve and avoid the figures, but his wife, despite braking hard rode straight into them, expecting to hit a solid object she was horrified to ride right through them. It was the shock of this that made her fall from her cycle. Her husband in the meantime had stopped and turned around, he saw the whole incident. The two figures carried on just as if nothing had happened and disappeared into a thick hedge!!

Ten years or more passed with nothing else being heard about this phenomena, until one day, two building workers were returning home along the same road in their car, when the passenger shouted to the driver to stop. He had seen a figure of a man crossing the road directly in front of them and he was certain that they were going to run him down. Later, he described the figure as wearing a long black raincoat and sou'wester hat, but strangely enough the driver saw nothing. But never-the-less, he stopped the car and they both got out and walked back along the road but could see nothing nor anybody. It then occurred to them that if they had hit somebody or something, they would have felt a bump, which neither had. So they came to the conclusion that the passenger had either dropped off to sleep and dreamt the whole episode or it must have been a ghost!!!

The writer of this story, hearing these stories from two different sources and realising that there was a similarity between them, decided to do some research on the matter.

After searching around for a long time for a lead, eventually found an elderly lady who recalled that when she was a young girl, her father had told her a strange story about this farmhouse.

In earlier days, the present farmhouse had been a small mansion that was occupied by a wealthy wool merchant who had a beautiful daughter who he adored. Now this girl was in love with a groom from the nearby Hall, much against her fathers wishes, as he considered that a groom being of a lower class was not a fitting companion for his daughter. So he forbade her to meet him, but being very much in love with each other they still continued to meet. Her father, finding that she was ignoring his views, decided to take the law into his own hands and put an end to the romance once and for all.

Waiting for a moonlight night, the old wool merchant took his blunderbuss and hid in the clump of trees and waited. He didn't have to wait for long. Across the road strode the tall groom to disappear into the far end of the trees. After a short while, the father saw a shadow outlined beside a tree, taking his chance, he raised the blunderbuss to his shoulder and took aim at the shadow and fired. But what he did not know was, that his dearly beloved daughter was in the arms of the unfortunate groom —- They died as they would have wished — tightly embraced in each others arms with their lips to each others!!!

If you have enjoyed reading HAUNTED CLACTON, watch out for further books in the WESLEY'S ESSEX COLLECTION.

Shortly to be published.

Stories of the Thorpe-le-Soken area.
Little Clacton Stories.
St. Osyth Legends and Stories.
Treasure Holt — Its Ghosts & Mysteries.
Etc. Etc. Etc.

The publishers would welcome any stories or experiences of Ghosts and Hauntings in Essex for future books.